Zen Pig

Book 7

Peaceful Protest

written by:

mark brown

illustrated by:

mariangela cinelli

Spread the love with...
#ZenPig

Dedicated to Jacquelyn,
the original Zen Pig superfan.

Your unwaivering support of this mission,
since day one, will not be forgotten.
I am forever grateful - thank you.

Zen Pig's heart had become heavy,
Some things in his town were just not right.
Just because everyone did not look the same,
Made a few people want to fight.

Quickly, Zen Pig acted,
He wanted to help without delay.
Peacefully gathering his neighbors and friends,
He knew this would be the best way.

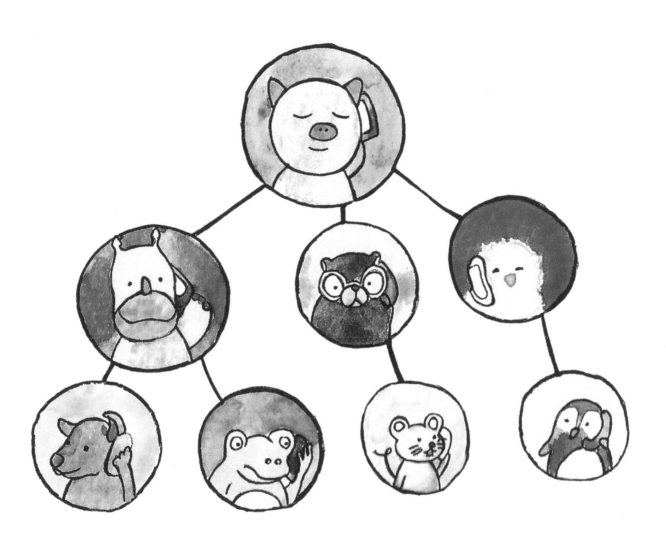

Coming together at the town center,
They all wanted to see the change.
Lifting homemade banners and signs,
The crowd listened to what Zen Pig had to say.

"My dear neighbors and friends,

Thank you for coming today.

It's important we stand up for those treated poorly,

By those who have lost their way.

Even though some look different than others,
We are all part of the beautiful whole.
Being unkind is never the answer,
Lifting each other up is our role.

When we choose to hurt others,
We are also hurting ourselves.
Our hearts must never become a place,
In which we allow hate to dwell.

With love, we must look unto each other,
With care, we must listen for cries.
We are only as good as the person in need,
We must ensure to help others rise.

In any group, there will be voices
That simply are not as loud.
We each have a duty to echo their words,
Until they are heard by the crowd.

If we see someone being treated
Unfairly and unjust,
Bravely, we must stand with them,
And tell those that we trust.

To ensure we all stand as equals,

We must help some to their feet.

With love, we offer both our hands

To everyone that we meet.

Together, we can accomplish
So much more than we can divided.
We must embrace and celebrate our differences
And from this moment on, be united.

Just like pieces to a puzzle,

We each have our unique shape.

But once we all come together,

A masterpiece we make.

Right here and right now,

What was once a crowd of 'you' and 'me',

Has become a very powerful force,

A singular, loving 'We'. "

Namaste.

("The light in me loves the light in you.")

Name: _____

Age: _____ Date: _____

Zen Pig's Question:

How would YOU like to change
the world for the better?

_____

_____

_____

_____

_____

CPSIA information can be obtained
at www.ICGtesting.com
Printed in the USA
LVHW072219050321
680712LV00003B/9

9 781953 177186